THE VIPER

Lisa Thiesing

Dutton Children's Books ✳ *New York*

Library of Congress Cataloging-in-Publication Data
Thiesing, Lisa.
The Viper! / by Lisa Thiesing.—1st ed.
p. cm.
Summary: Peggy receives a mysterious call from the
Viper, warning that he is coming in one year, with
repeated calls which count down the dwindling time
until his arrival.
ISBN 0-525-46892-7
[1.Fear—Fiction. 2. Humorous stories.] I. Title.
PZ7.T35615 Vi 2002
[E]—dc21   2001047141

Published in the United States 2002
by Dutton Children's Books,
a division of Penguin Putnam Books for Young Readers
345 Hudson Street, New York, New York 10014
www.penguinputnam.com
Designed by Ellen M. Lucaire
Printed in Hong Kong
First Edition
1 3 5 7 9 10 8 6 4 2

For Max—
who always protected me from vipers

On a Friday,

the phone rang.

"Hello," said Peggy.

A husky, dusky voice hissed,

"I am zee Viper.

I vill come in 1 year."

"The Viper? How odd!"

Peggy said to herself.

"1 year. Well, that's

12 whole months from now.

365 days. Not to worry."

The months passed.

All was well.

And then . . .

the phone rang.

"I am zee Viper.

I vill come in 1 month."

"Let's see,"

thought Peggy out loud.

"30 days has September,

April, June, and November."

"All the rest have 31,

except February, which has 28,

unless it's a leap year,

and then it has 29."

"What's a viper anyway,

I wonder?"

Peggy looked up the word.

"OK. Hmm.

Violet . . . violin . . .

Ah! *Viper*!

A fanged, poisonous snake!

Oh my!"

"Why in the world would

a fanged, poisonous snake

be calling me?

Oooh, I hate snakes!"

Peggy was in bed.

The phone rang.

"I am zee Viper.

I vill come in 1 veek."

Now Peggy was awake.

So she went downstairs.

"Might as well have

a little snack.

7 days to go."

Sunday, Monday, and Tuesday

were pretty quiet.

Peggy did her chores.

She had fun, too.

But on Wednesday . . .

17

"I am zee Viper.

I vill come in 3 days."

Peggy was getting nervous.

"That's Saturday!"

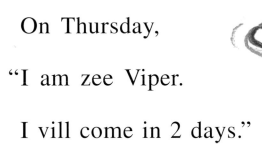

On Thursday,

"I am zee Viper.

I vill come in 2 days."

19

On Friday,

"I am zee Viper.

I vill come in 1 day."

Then, on Saturday,

"I am zee Viper.

I vill come at

12 o'clock."

"Noon! That's only

2 hours from now.

What to do?"

Set a trap!

String garlic around your neck!

Bolt the door!

Call the cops!

At 11 o'clock,

"I am zee Viper.

I vill come in 1 hour."

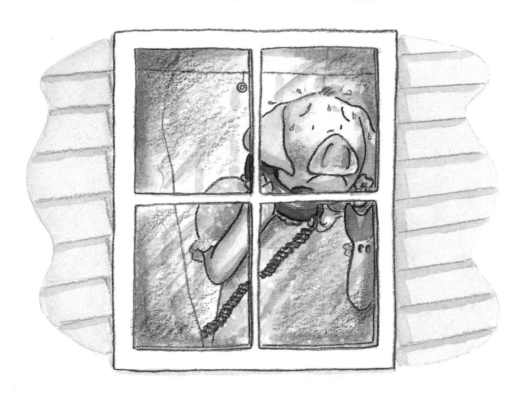

55 minutes later,

"I am zee Viper.

I vill come in 5 minutes."

4 minutes later,

"I am zee Viper.

I vill come in 1 minute."

Just 60 seconds left!

Hide!

Turn out the lights!

Peggy heard the creak of the fence . . .

the rattle of chains . . .

a slithering sound . . .

something,

someone, being dragged . . .

10, 9, 8, 7, 6, 5, 4, 3, 2, 1 . . .

"I am zee Viper.

I am at your door!"

Look through

the peephole,

if you dare . . .

"I am zee Viper," he said.

"I have come

to vipe your vindows!"

And so he did.